Sprite's
Secret

· by ·
TRACEY
WEST

A
LITTLE APPLE
PAPERBACK

SCHOLASTIC INC.
New York Toronto London Auckland Sydney
Mexico City New Delhi Hong Kong

This one's for the fairies.

—T. W.

Book design by Dawn Adelman

ISBN 0-439-17218-7

Sticker illustrations by James Bernardin
Interior illustrations by Thea Kliros

24 23 22 21 20 19 18   5/0

Printed in the U.S.A.   40
First Scholastic printing, May 2000

·· CONTENTS ··

In the back of Violet's house

There is an old oak tree.

In its trunk there is a door

Into our world, you see.

Fourteen pixies used that door

To flee their fairy home.

These pixies are quite tricky

And in our world they roam.

These pixies cause such trouble!

They must be stopped right now.

The fairy queen asked Sprite to help,

But he's not sure just how.

If these pixies are not caught,

What on Earth will be?

There is one way you can find out,

Read on and you will see!

Chapter One
A Marble, a Toad,
and a Fairy

"Give me back my marble!"

Violet Briggs was yelling at a toad. The toad hopped away from her. It held a large marble in its mouth.

It was Violet's favorite marble. The best one in her collection. She was in her backyard, playing with the marbles. Then the toad came. It picked up the marble and hopped away.

"Come back here!" Violet yelled.

Violet chased the toad. It hopped across the green grass. Violet reached for it. She almost had it. . . .

Hop! It landed on a rock.

Violet reached out again.

Hop! It landed in a patch of yellow buttercups.

Violet tried to grab it. . . .

Hop! The toad landed on the roots of an old oak tree.

Violet stopped running. She got down on her knees. The damp grass soaked through her jeans.

The toad sat still on the roots of the tree.

Slowly, Violet crawled to the toad.

"I don't want to hurt you," she whispered. "I just want my marble back!"

Violet held out her hand. She was so close! She could almost touch the toad's brown, bumpy skin.

Hop! The toad hopped right into a hole in the tree trunk and it disappeared.

"No!" Violet cried. She looked inside the hole.

A face looked back at her.

But it wasn't a frog face. In fact, it wasn't the face of an animal at all! It was the face of a tiny person.

Violet jumped back. The tiny person flew out of the hole. He floated in the air in front of Violet's face.

"Hello there," he said.

Violet tried to speak. But she couldn't. Not yet. She stared at the tiny creature.

He was about as tall as a pencil. He had green eyes that were tilted up a little bit. He had pointy ears. His skin was pale, pale green. And his hair was a very light yellow.

Violet thought his clothes were made from leaves. But the most amazing thing about him was his wings. They shimmered in the air. They looked like they were made of rainbows.

"I said, HELLO!" said the creature.

Violet closed her eyes. She *must* be seeing things.

Violet counted to three.

She opened her eyes.

The creature was still there.

"Are you all right?" he asked. His wings fluttered around her face.

"Are you a fairy?" Violet whispered.

"Yes," said the fairy. "They call me Sprite."

"I'm Violet," she said quietly.

"Are you eight years old?" Sprite asked.

Violet nodded slowly. How did he know *that*, she wondered.

Sprite grinned. He held out a large marble. "I think this belongs to you."

Violet didn't move. Was she really talking to a fairy? Could it be real?

She looked at Sprite carefully. There were no wires or strings holding him in the air. And he was solid, like a real thing. Not see-through like a cartoon character.

He must be real.

Violet slowly took the marble from the fairy's tiny hands.

"Thank you," Violet said.

"I'm glad I could help," Sprite said with a bow. "And now I need you to help me!"

"Me? How can I help you?" Violet asked.

She knew about fairies. She had read about fairies who gave out wishes. But she had never heard of a fairy who asked for help. Especially from an eight-year-old girl!

Sprite flew right up to Violet's face. His wings tickled her nose.

"You *must* help me," Sprite said. "Your world is in great danger!"

Chapter Two
Sprite's Story

"Hurry up! Put your sweater on. We must go. We've got to get started," Sprite said. He flew away from Violet.

Violet picked up her sweater and put it on. Wait a minute, she thought. I can't believe I'm actually listening to a fairy!

"Stop!" Violet called out.

Sprite made a quick turn in the air and zipped back to Violet.

"We can't stop!" Sprite said. "It's too important!"

Violet put her hands on her hips. "I'm not going anywhere with you," she said. "Not until you answer some questions."

Sprite sighed. He flew down and landed on a rock. Then he folded his wings behind him.

"I thought you said your name was Violet," Sprite said. "Violets are supposed to be quiet and shy. You're very loud, you know."

Violet frowned. "My name is Violet because of my eyes."

Sprite flew up to Violet's face. He blew a strand of dark hair away from her eyes.

"I see," Sprite said. "Your eyes are purple. Not like violets at all, though. More like gooseberries."

Violet brushed Sprite away. "Never mind about my name. Why is my world in danger?"

Excited, Sprite fluttered his wings. "It's just terrible! You see, yesterday some fairies escaped from my world. . . ."

"Your world?" Violet asked. "You mean in the oak tree?"

Sprite shook his head impatiently.

"The oak tree is just a door to my world," Sprite said. "I live in the Otherworld. With other creatures like me. You call us fairies. Or pixies."

"You mean like fairyland?" Violet asked.

"Yes! Yes!" Sprite said. "That's where I live. But some fairies escaped. Now they're here in your world, and I've got to bring them back!"

"What's the big deal about fairies escaping?" Violet asked. "You don't look very dangerous to me."

"Well, these fairies *are* dangerous,"

Sprite said. "And they don't all look like me. There are fourteen of them. They're all different. And by now they're probably making a huge mess of things. So we've got to find them right now!"

But Violet still wasn't convinced.

"Why do you have to catch these fairies all by yourself?" Violet asked.

Sprite puffed up his chest. He pulled a round medal from the bag that hung around his waist. He showed the medal to Violet. "I am a Royal Pixie Tricker. The queen chose me herself. Now, do you have any more questions, or can we go?"

Violet looked closely at the medal.

"One more question," Violet said, holding up her hand. "What's all this about a queen and you being a Royal Pixie Tricker? And why do you need *my* help?"

"The queen said I would meet an eight-year-old girl. She told me to ask you for help," Sprite said. "I'm not sure why. She said something about an old rhyme."

"Can't you remember?" Violet asked.

Sprite's wings fluttered impatiently.

"It's too long!" Sprite said. "And it doesn't matter. I found you, didn't I? So let's go!" He tugged on Violet's purple sweater.

"Not yet," Violet said.

"Not yet? What is it now?" Sprite asked.

"I can't just *leave*," Violet said. "I'm supposed to be playing in my backyard."

Violet pointed to the big yellow house in front of them.

"My aunt Anne is inside," Violet said. "It's Saturday. She always watches me when my parents work on the weekend."

"So tell Aunt Anne you have to go out," Sprite said.

"She'd never let me go running off with a fairy," Violet said.

"But this is important!" Sprite said. "I'm sure she'll understand."

Violet shook her head. "How could I tell her about you?" Violet asked. "She wouldn't believe me."

"I'll go introduce myself, then!" Sprite said.

"No!" Violet cried. She grabbed him by his tiny foot. "She'd hit you with a flyswatter. Or flush you down the toilet — or worse!"

"Boo-hoo-hoo! No help for you!"

Violet jumped at the sound of a strange voice.

The voice belonged to another fairy. He looked kind of like Sprite. But he was a bit taller. He didn't have any wings. He wore a cap with two points. There were bells on his pointy shoes.

"Pix!" Sprite yelled.

"Pix is my name, having fun is my game!" Pix sang. He danced in the grass. The bells on his shoes jingled.

Violet couldn't believe her eyes. Two fairies in one day?

Pix opened his hand. A pile of glittering dust appeared in his palm.

"Pix will dance, Pix will sing, Pix will trap you in a fairy ring!" Pix cried.

Pix blew the dust into the air. The dust whirled around. It formed a large circle and then surrounded Violet.

"Hey! What did you do?" Violet asked. She tried to walk through the shimmering ring, but she crashed into an invisible wall.

"It's no use, little girl," Pix said, grinning. "You're trapped in my fairy ring forever!"

Chapter Three
Pix!

"Don't worry, Violet!" Sprite yelled. "All you have to do is —"

"Not so fast!" Pix said. "Pix wants to play!"

Pix sprinkled some more pixie dust, and a jump rope magically appeared. And the rope was turning by itself!

Pix began jumping rope.

"This is fun!" Pix said. "Now your turn, Sprite!"

Sprite tried to fly away. But Pix made the jump rope twirl like a lasso. Suddenly, the rope wrapped around Sprite.

Pix grabbed the jump rope handle and pulled Sprite to the ground. Then he danced in circles around Sprite. Soon Sprite was completely tangled in the rope.

Violet banged her fists on the invisible wall. Nothing! She couldn't get out and help Sprite.

"Isn't jumping rope fun?" Pix asked Sprite.

Sprite couldn't answer. The rope covered his mouth.

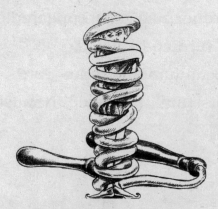

Pix frowned. "You don't like my game."

Pix yanked on the rope, and it unwound. Sprite's body twirled around and around.

Sprite was free of the rope. But he looked very dizzy.

"You'll really love this game!" Pix said. He opened his hand. A brightly colored ball appeared. "It's called dodgeball!"

Pix threw the ball at Sprite. Sprite fluttered his wings and flew out of the way.

Pix frowned. "I hate it when I miss!" he said.

Another ball appeared in Pix's hand. Pix threw the ball again. He missed. So Pix threw another ball. And another. Tiny dodgeballs flew everywhere.

Sprite flew around the yard, trying to dodge the balls. He looked exhausted.

"Violet, help!" Sprite called out.

"How can I?" Violet called back. "I'm trapped inside a fairy ring, remember?"

"Oh, right!" Sprite said. "It's easy to get out. All you have to do is —"

Sprite dodged another ball from Pix.

"Do what?" Violet yelled.

"Jump on one — no, that's not it," Sprite said. Another ball whizzed by him.

"What do I do?" Violet asked.

"You need to close your eyes — no, that's not it, either," Sprite said. He dodged another ball.

"Come on, Sprite!" Violet cried.

"Now I remember!" Sprite yelled. "Turn your sweater inside out. Then wear it backwards."

Violet wanted to ask how that was

supposed to get her out of the ring. But she knew there wasn't time. She quickly took off her sweater and turned it inside out. Then she put it on backwards.

Poof! The fairy ring vanished. Violet was free!

"That *was* easy," Violet said.

"Great!" said Sprite. "Now, can you please help me?"

Pix threw another ball at Sprite. Violet caught it just before it hit Sprite.

"Game's over, Pix!" she said.

Then Violet ran to the edge of the yard. She picked up a basketball that was lying there.

"I know how to play dodgeball, too," she said. "Can we play with *my* ball?"

The basketball was much bigger than Pix. Pix's eyes grew wide just looking at it.

"No, thanks," Pix said. He opened his

hand again and more glittery dust appeared. He threw the dust over his head.

"Catch you later!" Pix said. Then he disappeared.

Sprite flew to Violet's shoulder and sat down. "Thank you," he said. He sounded tired.

"Is that one of the fairies who escaped?" Violet asked.

Sprite nodded.

"Well, now I know why you were in such a hurry," Violet said. "Of course I'll help you!"

Chapter Four
Pixie Dust

Sprite fluttered his wings. "This is terrible," he said. "Pix is going to make a real mess of things."

"What will he do?" Violet said. "Play dodgeball with everybody?"

"It's much worse than that," Sprite said. "Pix loves to play. He wants everyone to play with him. He taps you on the head. Then you're under his spell. You'll want to play with him all the time."

"You mean you won't do homework? Or clean your room?" Violet asked.

Sprite nodded. "You won't eat. You won't sleep. You'll just play and play."

"That *is* bad," Violet said.

Sprite flew back and forth nervously. "So let's find him! Take me to a place where kids like to have fun. That's probably where he'll be."

"I will," Violet said. She put on her sweater the right way. "But not yet."

Sprite rolled his eyes. "What is it now?"

"I can't just leave my yard and walk all over town by myself," Violet said. "Aunt Anne will worry."

"Maybe *he* can come along and help us," Sprite said, flying over to a window in the house. Inside, there was a boy with sandy hair and freckles playing a video game.

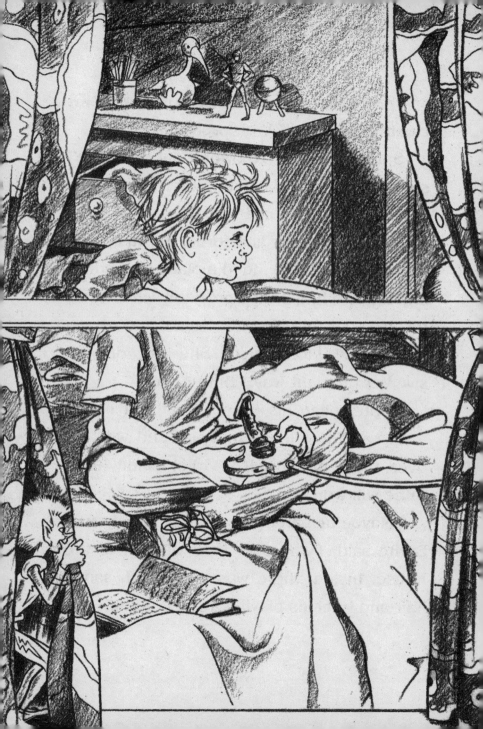

"No!" Violet said quickly. "That's my cousin Leon. He'd just spoil everything."

"Well, it doesn't matter," Sprite said. "I think I have something that will help."

Sprite opened the tiny bag that hung from his waist. He pulled out a handful of glittering dust.

Violet stepped back. "Are you going to trap me in a fairy ring with that?" she asked.

Sprite laughed. "No," he said. "I could if I wanted to. But pixie dust is good for lots of things, not just fairy rings."

"Like what?" Violet asked.

"I can sprinkle some on us. Then we can go anywhere we want in seconds," Sprite said. "Just like Pix did."

"Cool!" Violet said. "Then we can catch Pix fast. We'll be back before Aunt Anne misses me. And Leon won't see us leave."

"Right!" Sprite said. "So are you ready?"

"I think so," Violet said. "Does this stuff really work? I'm not going to disappear forever, am I?"

"It works just fine!" Sprite said. "Where should we go first?"

"Well, Pix likes dodgeball. Maybe we can go to a place where kids play ball," Violet said. "We can go —"

Sprite didn't wait for Violet to finish. He quickly blew the pixie dust over both of them.

At first, the dust just made Violet sneeze.

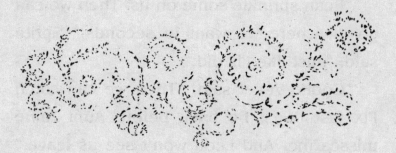

Then she felt her body tingle like a million tiny feathers were tickling her skin.

The backyard disappeared. Violet saw only white light.

Then the light faded and the tingling stopped.

Splash! Violet felt water sloshing in her shoes.

Violet blinked. They weren't at the *ball field*. They were at the *mall*.

Right in the middle of the wishing fountain!

Violet was standing knee-deep in water. A big statue of a fish squirted water on top of her head.

Sprite flew next to Violet's face. He was nice and dry.

"I said *ball*, not *mall*," Violet said. "How did we get here?"

Sprite shrugged. "Sorry," he said. "I'm kind of new at this."

"What do you mean?" Violet yelled. Then she heard a familiar laugh.

It was her friend Brittany Brightman.

Violet tried to duck behind the fish statue. She was too late.

"Violet!" Brittany cried. "What are you doing in the fountain?"

Chapter Five
Lost!

Violet had to think fast. If Brittany found out about Sprite, she'd tell everybody. Brittany was like that.

And Violet didn't know what would happen if other people found out about Sprite. They might be afraid. They might put Sprite in a jar. Or on a TV talk show.

So Violet grabbed Sprite and shoved him into her sweater pocket.

"Violet? What are you doing?" Brittany asked again.

"Hi, Brittany," Violet said. "I'm just uh . . . uh. . ."

"Taking a bath!" Sprite whispered.

"Taking a bath!" Violet said without thinking.

"Ha-ha," Brittany said. "Very funny, Violet."

Violet blushed. *That Sprite!*

"Just kidding," Violet said. "I, uh, I dropped something."

"Oh," Brittany said. She looked at her friend strangely. "You'd better get out of there. I think there are bugs in that fountain. I saw one flying near your head before."

Violet gasped. Brittany must have seen Sprite! But she thought he was a bug.

"Bugs. Right," Violet said. "Don't worry. I'll be fine."

"I've got to go," Brittany said. "I've been waiting forever to get someone to help me in the shoe store. The salesclerks are acting really weird today."

Brittany ran into the shoe store across from the fountain.

Violet crouched behind the fish statue. She pulled Sprite from her pocket.

Sprite frowned at Violet. He smoothed out his wings.

"What did you do that for?" he asked. "It was very cramped in there."

"I did it so no one would see you," Violet said. "We should try again. We have to find Pix."

"I think he might have been here," Sprite said. "Look."

Sprite pointed to the shoe store. The workers in the store weren't helping the customers. They were playing catch with a pair of slippers.

Angry customers yelled at them. But the workers didn't care. They kept on playing.

"Pix must have tapped them on the head," Sprite said. "He's working fast."

"So let's look for him," Violet said. She started to step out of the fountain.

A woman's voice blared over a loud-speaker.

"This is the mall manager," she said. "The mall is closed! No work today! Just play!"

"We're too late," Violet said.

"He must be headed somewhere else," Sprite said. He reached in his bag and pulled out more pixie dust. "Where should we go?"

"Maybe the playground," Violet said. "There are lots of games to play there."

Sprite blew the pixie dust on them. The fountain and the mall disappeared.

Violet sneezed. She closed her eyes.

When she opened them, all she saw was fog. Thick, gray fog.

Sprite flew in front of her. She could barely see him. All she could see were his shimmering wings.

"Where are we? What happened?" Violet asked. "Did you make another mistake?"

"No," Sprite said. "But I'm not sure what happened."

"Maybe we should try to get out of this fog," Violet said. "Sit on my shoulder so I don't lose you."

Violet felt Sprite land on her shoulder. Then she took a step forward. The thick fog swirled around them. Violet couldn't see a thing.

Violet took one step. Then another.

Then she stopped.

"This is no good," Violet said. "I don't even know where we are."

Sprite's tiny ears perked up. "Do you hear that?"

Violet listened. She thought she heard kids laughing and playing.

"I think we're near the playground," Sprite said.

"You might be right," Violet said. "So how did this fog get here? Did Pix do it?"

Sprite shook his head. "Pix can't do this kind of magic. But Hinky Pink could."

"Hinky who?" Violet asked.

"Hinky Pink. He's another fairy," Sprite said. "He can control the weather. He could be trying to keep us from catching Pix."

Violet shivered. The fog felt cold and clammy.

"Can't we undo the magic?" Violet asked. "I could turn my sweater inside out again."

"That won't do," Sprite said. "This magic is too strong for that."

"Then what can we do?" Violet asked.

"There is one thing," Sprite said. "We could try saying Hinky Pink's name backwards. Three times."

"Backwards?" Violet asked. She tried to picture the name in her mind. "You mean we have to say, 'Knip Yknih'?" Her tongue tripped over the words.

"That's it!" Sprite said. "But we have to do it together."

"Slowly!" Violet said.

Violet's and Sprite's voices rang out in the fog.

"Knip Yknih.

"Knip Yknih.

"Knip Yknih!"

A strong wind came. It blew the fog away.

Violet blinked. Now the sun shone brightly in her eyes. The sky was blue. There were no clouds in the sky. It was like magic!

And the playground was right in front of them.

"We did it!" Sprite said. Then he pointed at the playground. "And there's Pix!"

Chapter Six
Pix Power

"Quick! Let's hide!" Sprite said.

He flew behind a tree. Violet followed.

Sprite peeked out at the playground. It was crowded with children.

"What's Pix doing?" Violet asked.

"He tapped the children in the playground," Sprite said. "They're under his spell."

Violet peeked out from behind the tree.

Children were playing and laughing. They swung on the swings. They slid down the slide. They went around and around on the merry-go-round.

Pix sat on one end of a seesaw. A little boy sat on the other end. Pix laughed as the seesaw flew up and down.

Violet turned to Sprite. "I don't get it," she said. "They all look like they are having fun."

"Look closer," Sprite said.

Violet looked again. Then she understood. The kids didn't look happy. They all looked tired. Their eyes looked glazed, like they were sleepwalking.

"That's not normal," Violet said.

A mom ran up to a little boy on the swing. She tried to pull him off. But the little boy cried and shouted.

"No! No! I want to play!" the boy cried.

The mom looked worried. Then Pix hopped off the seesaw. He snuck up behind her. He tapped her on the head.

The mom laughed. She sat down on another swing.

"You're right! Let's play!" she said.

Violet frowned. "Pix is going to have everybody under his spell! How can we stop him?"

Sprite looked down at his pointy shoes. "I'm not really sure," he said.

"Not sure!" Violet said. "I thought you were a Royal Pixie Tricker."

Sprite blushed. But he didn't blush pink, he turned a brighter shade of green. "I *am* a Royal Pixie Tricker," he said. "But there's so much to remember. It all gets mixed up in my head."

Violet sighed. They had to think of a way to break Pix's spell.

"I know," Violet said. "What if we get everybody to turn their jackets inside out? And wear them backwards? It worked before."

Sprite looked troubled. "That could be it. But I'm not sure."

"It's worth a try," Violet said. "You can go to the playground. You can tell the kids what to do. You can whisper in their ears."

"All right," Sprite said. "I'll do it!"

"Wait a minute," Violet said.

Sprite flew back to her. He landed on a tree limb.

"I changed my mind," Violet told him. "Pix might see you if you go in there. Then he might do something to hurt you. Or turn you into something."

Sprite put his hands on his hips. "He can't harm me. I'm a Royal Pixie Tricker!"

"It's just that we don't have time to

waste," Violet explained. "We need to get this right. No mistakes this time."

"Well, we have to do something," Sprite said.

"I can go on the playground. If Pix spots me, I'll just pretend I'm one of the kids he put under his spell, " Violet said.

"Hmm. I don't know," Sprite said. "Pix has powerful magic.

"All right, Violet," Sprite said finally. "But be very careful. Good luck."

Violet stepped out from behind the tree.

She opened the playground gate and walked inside.

Chapter Seven
Under a Spell

Violet ran behind the slide.

She really didn't want Pix to see her.

But Pix didn't notice Violet at all.

He ran to the sandbox. He jumped in. He threw sand in the air and laughed.

Violet climbed up the ladder of the slide. A little girl sat on top. She looked about five years old.

Violet tugged on her jacket.

"Listen to me," Violet said. "You're under a spell. That pixie wants you to play forever."

The little girl just laughed, but she didn't look happy.

"I'm having fun!" she said. She slid down the slide, away from Violet.

Violet slid down after her.

Maybe some other kids would listen.

She walked to the merry-go-round. Two boys her age were pushing it.

"You're under a spell!" Violet told them. "Turn your jackets inside out. Then wear them backwards. You can break the spell!"

"Who cares?" said one of the boys.

"Get lost!" said the other.

They jumped on the merry-go-round.

Violet didn't know what to do.

No one wanted to listen to her. They were all under Pix's spell.

Violet stopped. She looked around her.

I have to do something, Violet thought. But what?

Then something tickled Violet's nose. Pixie dust!

Violet sneezed.

Something whipped by her face. Something with shoes with bells on them.

Oh, no! Pix!

"Violet!" Sprite called out.

Violet turned. Sprite was flying next to the playground gate. He looked worried. Violet ran over to him.

"Pix was about to tap you!" Sprite said. "I had to let you know, so I sprinkled pixie dust on you."

Then Violet knew what had happened. Her sneeze must have kept Pix from tapping her. He had almost put her under his spell!

"Thanks, Sprite," Violet said.

"Watch out!" Sprite yelled.

Violet spun around.

Pix jumped off a swing. He started to dance. He danced closer and closer to Violet.

"Soon you'll play with me forever!" he said in a singsong voice.

Violet thought fast. Then she had an idea.

I'll just say Pix's name backwards. Three times, Violet thought. Just like with Hinky Pink.

Violet pointed at Pix.

"Xip! Xip! Xip!" she yelled loudly.

Chapter Eight
The *Book of Tricks*

Nothing happened.

Pix laughed and laughed.

"You've come to stop me," he said. "But it won't be so easy this time!"

Pix tugged at the leg of Violet's jeans. "Come and play! Have fun with Pix!"

Violet shook her leg. Pix tumbled off.

Violet ran back to the playground gate. "The backwards magic didn't work!" Violet told Sprite. "It worked on Hinky Pink."

Sprite's wings fluttered nervously.

"I don't know why it didn't work," Sprite said. "Maybe this is strong magic. Even stronger than Hinky Pink's fog."

"What kind of a Royal Pixie Tricker are you?" Violet asked. "Don't you know what to do?"

Sprite avoided Violet's eyes. "I *do* know what to do," he muttered. "It's on the tip of my wings. . . ."

Then he smiled. "Of course! The book!"

Sprite dug into the bag around his waist. He pulled out a tiny book with a gold cover.

Violet leaned over and looked at the book. She could just make out the title.

"*Book of Tricks*," she said. "What is it?"

"There's only one way to send a fairy back to the Otherworld," Sprite said. "With a trick."

"A trick from that book?" Violet asked.

Sprite nodded. "There's a different trick for each fairy."

"Why didn't you think of this sooner?" Violet asked.

Sprite blushed bright green again. "I told you. I'm sort of new at this."

Sprite opened the book. He turned the pages quickly.

"Pix . . . Pix," Sprite said. "Oh, here it is! It's in rhyme." Sprite read the poem out loud.

"'Pix loves nothing more than fun.
Give him some work, and his fun is done!'"

"Give him some work," Violet said. "You mean we have to make Pix work? Like do a chore?"

"Yes," Sprite said.

"And then what happens?" Violet asked.

"Then Pix will be sent back to the Otherworld," Sprite said. "The spell will be broken."

Violet felt a little better. It was nice to know exactly what to do.

There was only one problem.

"How are we supposed to get Pix to do a chore?" Violet asked. "All he wants to do is play."

Chapter Nine
Tricking Pix

"I'll think of something," Sprite said.

Pix ran up to Violet.

"There's no way to escape! Play with Pix instead," he cried.

Pix gave Violet a big shove. She flew through the air. Like magic. Then she landed on the seesaw.

"Ow!" Violet yelled.

Pix hopped on the other end of the seesaw.

"Pix loves the seesaw!" he cried. "Up and down! Up and down!"

Violet felt sick to her stomach. They were going too fast.

But how could she stop Pix? She had to trick him.

"Up and down! Up and down!" Pix yelled.

Then it came to her.

"Sprite!" she called out. Sprite flew over to her. Violet whispered in his ear, "Keep Pix busy. I know what to do."

"Got it!" Sprite said, and flew away.

Sprite yelled at Pix. "Hey, Pix! Come over here!"

Pix hopped off the seesaw. He ran over to Sprite.

"What is it, loser?" Pix asked Sprite. "You'd better stop trying to catch me. It's no use."

"I know," Sprite said. "I just thought you'd like to see a cool trick."

Sprite took a gold yo-yo from his magic bag. He dangled the yo-yo in front of Pix. Then Sprite made the yo-yo spin in circles.

Pix's eyes lit up. "Give it to me! Pix wants to play!"

Sprite threw the yo-yo to Pix. Pix started doing tricks with it.

Violet saw Pix playing with the yo-yo. She had to move fast.

Violet jumped off the seesaw. She looked around the playground.

She found what she was looking for. A broken branch from a tree. It was small and thick. Just perfect.

Violet ran back to the seesaw. It was empty.

She stuck the tree branch in the middle of the seesaw. She put it right in the part that helps the seesaw go up and down.

Then she yelled, "Oh, no! The seesaw's broken!"

Some of the kids ran up to her. They tried to move the seesaw up and down.

It was stuck.

One of the little kids began to cry.

Pix heard the noise. He threw down the yo-yo.

"What's this?" he asked. "No crying. Time to play with Pix!"

"But the seesaw's broken," Violet said. "We can't play."

Pix shrugged. "So what? There are other things to play on."

"But the seesaw's the best thing in the whole playground," Violet said.

Pix raised his eyebrows. "It is? Why?"

"Because you get to play with someone else," Violet replied.

"That's right," Pix said. "I don't like to play alone."

"It's too bad," Violet said. "Because the seesaw's broken."

Pix ran to the seesaw. "I'll see about that!" he said.

Pix climbed up to the end of the seesaw. He jumped up and down.

The seesaw didn't move.

"Drat!" Pix said.

Pix hopped off the seesaw. He walked underneath.

"Here's the problem," Pix said. "There's a tree branch stuck here."

Pix grabbed the tree branch. He pulled and pulled.

Suddenly, the branch came loose.

"I did it!" Pix said. "I fixed the seesaw."

Violet did it! She made Pix do a chore!

Then a cold wind kicked up. The wind

blew all over the playground. Violet's hair whipped around her face.

The wind formed a tunnel in the air. Right behind Pix.

The wind tunnel swirled and swirled. The wind pulled Pix back, back into the tunnel.

"Pix doesn't like this game!" Pix cried.

The wind pulled Pix farther into the tunnel.

The tunnel closed up.

Then it disappeared.

Pix was gone!

Chapter Ten
One Down

The kids in the playground looked funny. Like they had just woken up. They slowly walked off the playground.

The spell was broken!

"Did we really do it?" Violet asked. "Did we send Pix back to the Otherworld?"

Sprite opened the *Book of Tricks*. Next to Pix's rhyme was a blank page.

Violet watched as a picture slowly formed on the page. It was a picture of Pix.

Pix

Pix loves
nothing more
than fun
Give him some
work
and his
fun is done

"What does it mean?" Violet asked.

"When Pix escaped, his picture disappeared from the book," Sprite explained.
"Now it's here. It means we sent Pix back."

"Good!" Violet said. She watched as Sprite
closed the book.

"That's one down, thirteen to go."

"Right!" Sprite said. "So we should get
moving."

"Hold on," Violet said. "We can't look for
pixies now."

"We can't?" Sprite asked. "Why not?"

"Aunt Anne will be calling for me," Violet said. "It's almost time for dinner. Then I take a bath. And then I go to bed."

Sprite sighed. "You humans have so many rules."

"The pixies will just have to wait," Violet said.

"Maybe," Sprite said. "Or maybe not."

Sprite pointed to something just above Violet's head.

Violet looked up. A black cloud hung in the air. But the rest of the sky was sunny and blue.

Cold raindrops fell from the cloud. Right on Violet's head.

Violet groaned. "Let me guess," she said. "Hinky Pink!"

Sprite tried to hide a smile. He flew outside the raindrops.

"See, Violet," Sprite said, "the pixies won't rest until we trick them all!"

Pixie Tricks Stickers

Use the stickers with your *Book of Tricks*. When Sprite and Violet catch a pixie, stick its sticker in the book. Follow the directions in the *Book of Tricks* to complete each pixie's page. (Pixie Secret: Most of these pixies haven't been caught yet. Save their stickers to use later.)

PiXiE TRiCKS

_____'s

(YOUR NAME)

Book of Tricks

Sprite has his Book of Tricks.
Now you have your very own, too!

Use this book each time Violet and Sprite
catch a pixie. Here's what you do:

1. Put the pixie's sticker next to its name.

2. Write when Sprite and Violet sent the
pixie back to the Otherworld.

3. Write the magic rhyme from Sprite's Book
of Tricks. It tells how to trick the pixie.

4. One sticker shows something the pixie
put a spell on. Put that sticker in the book.
For example, Pix put a spell on a dodgeball
in the first book, so you would put the
dodgeball sticker on Pix's page.

5. One sticker shows what Violet and Sprite used to trick the pixie. Put that sticker in the book, too. For example, Violet and Sprite used a seesaw to trick Pix in the first book, so you would put the seesaw on Pix's page.

Hint 1: You might not have all the stickers you need at first. Look for the other stickers you need in later Pixie Tricks adventures!

Hint 2: Read the labels next to the stickers on the sticker page. These labels will help you figure out where each sticker should go.

When you've collected all the stickers and filled in this book, you'll be a Royal Pixie Tricker. Just like Sprite.

Good luck!

The Poem from the Fairy Queen's Book

If ever pixies do escape

Through the old oak tree,

Here is what you have to do

Or trouble there will be.

First find a Pixie Tricker,

The youngest in the land.

Send him to the human world,

The *Book of Tricks* in hand.

Once he's there he'll find a girl

Who's only eight years old.

But she's a smart and clever girl

Who's also very bold.

He must ask her for her help

And if she does agree,

They'll trick the pixies, one by one

Till no more do they see.

Only they can do the job.

It's much more than a game.

For if they fail to trick them all

The world won't be the same!

How to Find an Escaped Pixie

Tracking down pixies can be tricky. You could search and search and never find one. Or one could pop up in front of your nose when you least expect it! You never know what a pixie will do!

People have all kinds of ideas about how to find pixies.

• Some people look at dawn and sundown, or at noon and midnight. Pixies like the in-between times, when it's not quite morning or afternoon, and neither day nor night.

- A ring of mushrooms growing out of the ground could be a sign of a pixie ring.

- Pixies love wild places in nature. Look in woods, meadows, and around mountains.

- Pixies often gather where two points meet. Where the ocean meets the sand or where one road meets another are good places to see pixies.

- Pixies love flowers and trees. That butterfly you've seen flitting around your garden might be a pixie in disguise!

How to Trick a Pixie

You now know where to look for a pixie. But what should you do when you find it?

To send an escaped pixie back to the Otherworld, you have to trick it. The best way to trick a pixie is to get it to do something different than it usually does. For example, to trick a pixie that always lies, you would have to get it to tell the truth.

Here are some famous pixies who once escaped into the human world. A Royal Pixie Tricker tricked them and they were sent back. Can you figure out how they were tricked? Take this quiz to find out.

Weepy was a gnome who cried all the time. How do you think Weepy was tricked? _____

_____

Zzzeke was an elf who slept late every morning.

How do you think Zzzeke was tricked? _____

_____

Cavity was a troll who never brushed his teeth.

How do you think Cavity was tricked? _____

_____

Turn the page upside down for the answers.

How did you do? If you got all three right, you're ready to start tricking pixies!

To trick Weepy, you have to make her laugh; to trick Zzzeke, you have to wake him up early; to trick Cavity, you have to make him brush his teeth or go to the dentist.

Pixie Trickers
Sprite

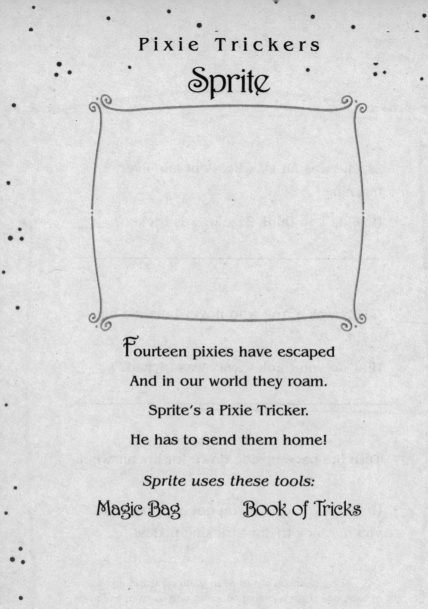

Fourteen pixies have escaped

And in our world they roam.

Sprite's a Pixie Tricker.

He has to send them home!

Sprite uses these tools:

Magic Bag   Book of Tricks

Pixie Trickers
Violet

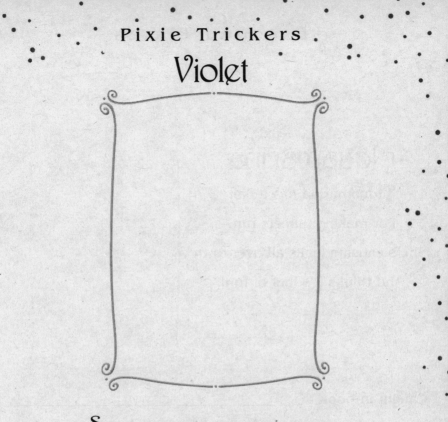

Sprite will need to find some help,

Someone who's smart and bold.

He will ask a little girl,

Who's only eight years old.

She must give Sprite her word.

She'll help him take a stand.

Then they'll trick the pixies

And return them to their land.

Aquamarina

Aquamarina has a flair

For making faucets run.

She's causing leaks all over town

And thinks it's lots of fun!

Caught in book #: _____

Magic rhyme: _____

_____

Aquamarina put a spell on this: The Pixie Trickers used
                                     this to trick Aquamarina:

Bogey Bill

Creepy critters, slimy snakes,

A really scary dream.

This freaky goblin will try it all

Just to hear you scream.

Caught in book #: _____

Magic rhyme: _____

_____

Bogey Bill put a spell on this:

The Pixie Trickers used this to trick Bogey Bill:

Escaped Pixies
Buttercup

Hiccups in the morning, hiccups in the night.

If you've got the hiccups, then Buttercup's in sight.

Caught in book #: _____

Magic rhyme: _____

_____

Buttercup put a spell on this: The Pixie Trickers used
                                       this to trick Buttercup:

Fixit

Here's a special warning

To all you girls and boys:

Fixit can be nasty

When making all your toys!

Caught in book #: _____

Magic rhyme: _____

_____

Fixit put a spell on this: The Pixie Trickers used
                                        this to trick Fixit:

Greenie and Meanie

Watch out for your pets, with these two dwarves around.

They'll take them far away, where pets cannot be found.

Caught in book #: _____

Magic rhyme: _____

_____

Greenie and Meanie
put a spell on this:

The Pixie Trickers used this
to trick Greenie and Meanie:

Hinky Pink

If it's raining when the sun is out,

Then Hinky Pink is near.

He can make it rain or snow,

And then he'll disappear.

Caught in book #: _____

Magic rhyme: _____

_____

Hinky Pink put a spell on this:

The Pixie Trickers used
this to trick Hinky Pink:

Escaped Pixies

Jolt

Jolt likes a gadget,

Jolt loves a game.

But once he gets a hold of it,

It will not be the same.

Caught in book #: _____

Magic rhyme: _____

_____

Jolt put a spell on this:

The Pixie Trickers used
this to trick Jolt:

Escaped Pixies
Pix

No more homework, no more chores,

Everyone must play.

That's the way the world would be

If Pix had things his way.

Caught in book #: _____

Magic rhyme: _____

_____

Pix put a spell on this: The Pixie Trickers used
                                        this to trick Pix:

Ragamuffin

Once you had two striped socks,

But one vanished into thin air.

With Ragamuffin on the prowl,

One foot is always bare.

Caught in book #: _____

Magic rhyme: _____

_____

Ragamuffin put a spell on this: The Pixie Trickers used
                                    this to trick Ragamuffin:

Rusella

If there are mixed-up messages

And everything's confused,

Rusella might be playing games.

That's how she stays amused.

Caught in book #: _____

Magic rhyme: _____

_____

Rusella put a spell on this:

The Pixie Trickers used
this to trick Rusella:

Spoiler

When everything seems perfect,

When everything seems right,

You can sure bet Spoiler,

Will wreck it all for spite.

Caught in book #: _____

Magic rhyme: _____

_____

Spoiler put a spell on this:

The Pixie Trickers used
this to trick Spoiler:

Sport

No shots, no goals, no points,

You just can't win the game?

If the rules just don't seem fair,

Maybe Sport's to blame!

Caught in book #: _____

Magic rhyme: _____

_____

Sport put a spell on this: The Pixie Trickers used
                                     this to trick Sport:

Escaped Pixies
Finn

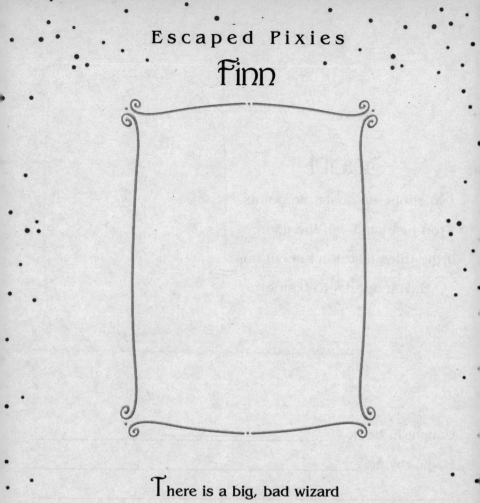

There is a big, bad wizard

With an evil, nasty grin.

He helped the pixies all escape.

His name is Wizard Finn.

First seen in book #: _____

A Friend Indeed
Robert B. Gnome

Robert lives in the human world,

Where he's a garden gnome.

He'll help the Trickers find out how

To send the pixies home.

First seen in book #: _____

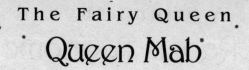

The Fairy Queen
Queen Mab

Queen Mab protects the Otherworld.

She's brave and wise and nice.

She helps trick the pixies

By sharing sage advice.

The Pixie Code

It's not easy to track a pixie. If you are working with a friend, you might need to keep your messages secret.

Use the code wheel on the next page to keep your messages safe from prying pixie eyes. Here's how it works:

1. Write your message:

> I HAVE FOUND THE PIXIE.

2. Start with the first letter. Find the letter on the outside wheel. Then see what letter it matches up with on the inside wheel. That is your code letter: I = A

3. Write the rest of your message using the code wheel:

4. Give a copy of the code wheel to your friend. Tell your friend to look up each letter on the inside of the wheel and match it to the letter on the outside of the wheel. Then your friend can decode the message:

A MFNH BDTSL IMH ZAOAH.

I HAVE FOUND THE PIXIE.

Your Page

Your name: _____

Age: _____

Favorite Pixie Tricker: _____

Favorite escaped pixie: _____

Favorite Pixie Tricks book: _____

If you could invent a magic tool to help

Sprite and Violet, what would it be? _____

_____

Congratulations!

I HEREBY GIVE

_____

(Your name here)

THE TITLE OF Royal Pixie Tricker

FOR TRICKING ALL FOURTEEN PIXIES

AND SENDING THEM BACK

TO THE OTHERWORLD.

The next time you're out walking

On a bright and sunny day,

Remember all you've read

About the pixie way.

Keep your eyes wide open,

And take your steps with care.

For if you're very lucky,

You might see a pixie there.